To the Max

SCHOLASTIC
SYDNEY AUCKLAND NEW YORK TORONTO LONDON MEXICO CITY
NEW DELHI HONG KONG BUENOS AIRES PUERTO RICO

WELCOME

Enter the *X•Zone*!

Every ***X•Zone*** book is full of facts and amazing true stories that will take you around the world and back.

You'll find vivid photos and illustrations that will spark your imagination.

One thing to keep in mind: If you see a word in **bold**, look in the glossary for the meaning!

Ready for an adventure in reading?

Then enter the ***X•Zone!***

Contents

What is an ollie?

PAGE **6**

What are the Planet X World Games?

PAGE **20**

Who were the first bungee jumpers?

PAGE **25**

TO THE MAX

Taking **Sports** *to the* **Extreme**

Extreme sports involve danger and high risk. Most action sports can be made extreme with the use of different equipment, the invention of new and more difficult stunts, and greater risk-taking. New sports are being invented that move out of the safety zone and into the danger zone.

Because of the dangers involved extreme athletes have to take extra care to make sure they are not badly injured. This might involve wearing special clothing with extra padding in case of a fall. Extreme athletes train every day. To be the best and avoid injury requires many, many hours of practice.

Feel the Fear!

Extreme athletes get their thrills by pushing their sport and their bodies to the very limit of their ability. They are very skilful athletes. These thrill-seekers talk about the special feeling of *going to the max*, and getting that adrenalin rush. They crave excitement through maximum danger and maximum risk.

FACTS

Have you ever been really scared or in danger? At times like this the body produces a chemical called **adrenaline.** *Adrenaline makes the heart beat faster and improves your* ***reflexes****. It is the way your body prepares you for action.*

Bust a jib
When you have success with one of your tricks, you can say you've busted a jib.

Fakie
When you do a stunt and land facing backwards, that's a fakie.

I wonder what amazing new water sport someone will dream up next? Can you think of one?

WILD WATER

Extreme Summer

In summer, extreme athletes head for their skates, bikes, and boards. Some take to the water for their thrills. Let's take a look at some extreme summertime sports.

Wakeboarding

Have you ever watched a really fast speedboat? That huge trail of water speedboats leave behind them is called a ***wake***. Now imagine being towed behind that speedboat on a surfboard! In 1985 a man named Tony Finn (bottom right) designed a special board that was a cross between a water-ski and a surfboard.

This is how most extreme sports are created. Tony Finn was an inventor with a new idea.

He called his board a *skurfer*, and a new sport called *wakeboarding* was born. Wakeboarders can do daring tricks like jumps, turns, and rolls. Like skateboarding or snowboarding on water—that's wakeboarding!

In extreme wakeboarding, there are obstacles in the water, like kickers, ramps and sliders that launch wakeboarders high into the air.

The world record for inverts on a wakeboard is 15 in one minute.

FEATS

One of the most exciting wakeboarding tricks is called the double up. The speedboat makes a circle so that two wakes meet and double in size. Riders can jump an awesome 6 metres doing this trick! That's called taking air!

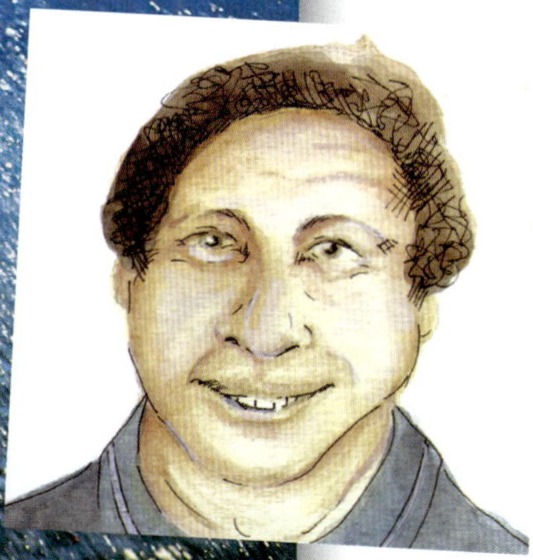

Tony Finn

Ollie

When you use your own energy to jump the board and land again, you've just done an ollie!

STREET STUNTS

You'll need a BMX bike, a street luge or a skateboard for street stunts. There are two types of skateboarding: street skate and **vert** skate.

Street Skating

Street skating is the most difficult and can take years to learn. You'll find street skaters out testing their skills in parks and on concrete surfaces. Stairs, handrails and benches add to the challenge. You could do an ollie to jump up on to a stair railing, **noseslide** down the rail and take air before you land back on the ground.

Extreme skaters add to the danger and risk by doing gap jumps on their skateboards. This involves jumping in the air from one obstacle to another. The bigger the gap between the obstacles, the more scary and risky the gap jump.

In 2000, skateboarding legend Andy Macdonald broke his own world record for gap jumping when he cleared an amazing 17.3 metres (57 feet).

Vert **Skating**

Gnarly
An awesome trick or obstacle is described as gnarly.

Vert skaters take to their boards on a special ramp or vert. The ramp looks like a pipe cut in half, so it's also called a halfpipe ramp. The ramp has vertical sides connected by a rounded surface called a *transition*. The top edge of the vertical sides is called the *coping*. You can perform some awesome tricks from the coping.

Extreme vert skaters launch themselves high in the air above the halfpipe, and test their skills and courage with breathtaking **aerial** stunts.

At the Summer X Games in 1999, champion skateboarder Tony Hawk launched into the air and performed the first "900" ever in vert skating. This means he turned his body 900 degrees which equals two and a half rotations. That's extreme!

Tony Hawk and Andy Macdonald

How do these guys do it? I still need lots more practice!

globe

STREET STUNTS

BMX *Riding*

BMX riders compete in street and vert events much like skateboarders. **Freestyle** BMX bikes have special rods or pegs called *grind pegs* attached to the front and back wheels. The grind pegs grind along the coping and other obstacles. Extreme riders use these pegs to perform daring backflips, "900"s, spins, and grinds.

In the vert events the bikes can **soar** up to three metres into the air. Extreme riders really get an adrenaline rush in the spectacular vert doubles competition, in which two riders perform on the halfpipe, twisting and spinning into the air at the same time. Awesome!

FACTS

BMX *stands for* bicycle motocross. *BMX bikes have smaller wheels and fatter tyres than other bikes. This makes them easier to control, especially on dirt tracks. BMX bikes are naturals for daredevils who want to ride to the max.*

Street Luge

Have you ever watched the luge competition at the Winter Olympics? A luge is a small one-person sled. In the luge event at the Olympics, athletes compete to see who is the fastest. They race on a special, very steep track. The luge is one of the fastest and most dangerous events at the Olympics.

Street luge was first tried by extreme skateboarders experimenting with new ways to test their skills. They tried lying on their boards and racing at high speeds down steep windy hills. Just like the luge at the Olympics but without the snow!

FACTS

Street luge is one of the world's fastest non-motorised sports

The street luge can be up to 2.6 metres (8.5 feet) long. Street luge riders are called *pilots*.

The pilot lies on a seat pan moulded to fit his or her body. Pilots steer the luge by leaning in the direction they want to go. Street luges can race as fast as 130 kph, with the pilot lying no more than five centimetres from the ground! For protection, pilots wear full-face helmets, padded leather suits and gloves, and thick-soled shoes. Even so, they risk serious injury if they crash or fall.

LINGO

Snocats
Don't expect a pussy cat in the snow! A snocat is a powerful motorised vehicle used to transport skiers.

ON THE ICE

If you thought summer extreme sports were hot just wait until you see the cool action in winter!

Snowboarding

There are two types of snowboards, freeriding boards built for speed, and freestyle boards built to show off your tricks.

Extreme freeriders compete in a race called the *King and Queen of the Hill*. This is the world championship of snowboarding and is held in Alaska, USA. A helicopter takes the thrill-seeking competitors to the top of a high snow-covered mountain. The freeriders **hurtle** down the steep slopes at breathtaking speeds. The first to the bottom wins!

Extreme freestyle riders choose the slopes or the half-pipe to show off their skills. Snowboarding tricks are similar to skateboard tricks. You'll see amazing spins, flips and grabs on the snow slopes, and a halfpipe built from snow.

The ultimate thrill in extreme snowboarding is Big Air. It's just one massive jump. Snowboarders hit the ramp, throw some amazing tricks and then try to land without falling over. When you *stick* your landing it means you have made it. One wrong move and it could end in disaster!

FEATS

In the Big Air competition some tricks sound more like menu items at a restaurant! This is chicken salad air! Why don't you find out about roast beef air or a mashed potato?

LINGO

Misty
A misty is when you spin and land facing to the front

Rodeo
Spin and land facing backwards

ON THE ICE

Freeskiing

Freeskiers take downhill skiing to the max. They get their adrenalin rush by finding the highest mountains and the steepest slopes, then skiing down them at top speeds. They face lots of hidden dangers, like sudden drops, or huge rocky boulders.

To perform tricks freeskiers often use special skis with twin tips. These skis are perfect for landing jumps forwards and backwards. Watch out for a *misty* or even a *rodeo*!

Extreme freeskiers need lots of courage and very fast reflexes!

Extreme freeskiers can get to the mountain tops the hard way by climbing the mountains. They are called ski mountaineers. *Some take the easy way up and use snocats. This is called* catskiing. *Sometimes they fly to the top in a helicopter. This is called* heli-skiing.

Knobbies *are tyres with extra tread for mud and off-road riding*

ON THE ICE

Biker X— Snow Mountain Biking

Imagine riding your mountain bike down a steep, snow-covered slope at over 96 kilometres an hour ... with no brakes! Scary, right? That's Biker X.

This is what it can feel like trying to stop at that speed on soft snow or slippery ice.

Snow mountain bikes are fitted with special snow tyres with metal studs, screws or even nails to help them grip onto slippery surfaces. The bikes also have large springs in the frame to absorb the shock after landing a big jump. This can help prevent the rider from being injured in a fall. The riders must wear suits with extra padding, gloves and helmets. There are plenty of falls and spectacular crashes in Biker X!

Biker X is one of the newest winter extreme sports. It was introduced at the 1999 Winter X Games in Colorado, USA. Six riders compete in a Biker X race. The downhill course has tight twists and turns and challenging jumps. Imagine six bikes hitting a corner at the same time! You're sure to see some spectacular crashes when you watch a Biker X race.

Competing *in the* ***Extreme***

Imagine the atmosphere of excitement and tension when extreme athletes get together to compete.

Their skills and courage are tested to the max at the Planet X World Games and the Gravity Games. There are Summer and Winter Games. During the games you can see the world's best extreme athletes compete. The summer events include BMX biking, freestyle motocross, street luge, skateboarding, inline skating and wakeboarding.

Millions of people around the world tune in to watch the thrills and spills of these extreme events.

New sports can always be added to the X Games. At the 2000 Winter Games there was a new event called *ultracross*. In ultracross, skiers and snowboarders compete as a team in a relay.

Women's Singles Luge medal winners from Germany.
2002 Winter Olympic Games, Salt Lake City.

Thrusty

A really difficult rock climb is called a thrusty *climb.*

THRILL SEEKING

New tricks, new thrills and new extreme sports are always being created. Let's take a look at a few new sports, and sports that are strictly for the ultimate thrill-seeker.

Rock Climbing

You need courage and **flexibility** to climb up a steep rock face. Rock climbers also have to think very carefully. There may be times when they need to make life-or-death decisions.

The most popular form of rock climbing is called *trad climbing*. This is when two climbers work together as a team to scale a cliff face. They use incredible strength in their arms and legs as well as special ropes and tools. As they climb, one climber fixes pegs into cracks in the rock. This lead climber then attaches a rope to a metal safety device called a ***karabiner***. The second climber follows the lead and removes the safety equipment. If you slip, the safety equipment will stop you from falling.

Climbers also use what they find on the rock face to help them climb. They might look for *buckets*. These are good places to hang on while you decide what your next move is.

Freeclimbing, or soloing is where a climber uses no equipment, just their own strength and skill. With no tools or ropes, buckets would be very important! Freeclimbing is the ultimate extreme test for a rock climber.

There are many other dangers for rock climbers, not just the risk of falling! They need to watch out for sunstroke, **dehydration** and muscle cramps.

FEATS

Rock-climbing legend Lynn Hill has freeclimbed a rock face, called The Nose of El Capitan. *The climb took her 23 hours! Lynn has won 30 international championships.*

Bridges are a favourite place for bungee jumping.

THRILL SEEKING

Bungee Jumping

You may be surprised to know that bungee jumping is not a new sport. It began hundreds of years ago as a tradition called *land diving* on Pentecost Island in the South Pacific. The islanders built towers of bamboo, wood and vines that were 30 metres tall.

To prove their bravery, young men would dive from the top of the towers with just a vine tied around their ankles. A trusted village elder chose the length and strength of the vine. There were no nets and no safety harnesses, just a vine to keep them from crashing to the ground. Land diving is still practised on Pentecost Island today.

Since the 1970s bungee jumping has become a popular extreme sport. Because of the danger involved, there are strict safety rules in place. For that extra adrenalin rush, some daredevils perform bungee stunts, doing flips and twists as they plunge from bridges, cranes and buildings.

FEATS

In 1980, David Kirk bungee jumped from a 320 metre high bridge in Colorado, USA.

In 1998, 25 people bungee jumped together in a mass jump from a height of 50 metres in Frankfurt, Germany.

LINGO

Dirt dive
A practise skydiving routine performed on the ground is called a dirt dive.

Skysurfing

Want to go skysurfing? You'll need to catch a plane, not a wave, and make sure your parachute is secure! Skysurfing is a cross between skateboarding and skydiving. At around 4000 metres the skysurfer jumps from a plane with a surfboard strapped to their feet. During the free fall the skysurfer performs spectacular rolls, spins and twists. Skysurfing is exciting to watch, but it's very dangerous to perform. It requires a lot of training and years of practice.

These dirt dives are coming together. Next step—the real thing!

Kitesurfing

Imagine being **harnessed** to a large kite and zooming through the surf on your board, with the wind pushing you to speeds of up to 25 knots (46kph/29mph)! At this speed kitesurfers can get really high and perform radical stunts to test their skills and courage. Kitesurfing is another dangerous sport that requires a high level of skills and many hours of practice.

What does the future hold for extreme sports? Will people take even greater risks to test the limits of extreme? What will people dream up next to go to the max? Maybe one day some extreme action sports will take place in space! What do you think?

FACTS

Skysurfers call falling upside down while spinning a helicopter spin. *The world record for helicopter spins is 64 spins in 20 seconds!*

Quiz

1 A *double up* is when
- a) two people ride on a bike
- b) you jump up in the air two times
- c) two wakes meet and double in size
- d) you do a trick twice

2 BMX stands for Bicycle Motocross.
True/False?

3 A luge is a
- a) small one person sled
- b) type of bicycle
- c) snowboard stunt
- d) large jet ski

4 Catskiing is
- a) skiing backwards
- b) walking up hill on skis
- c) a ski stunt
- d) getting up a mountain on a snocat

5 Street skaters use a special ramp called a halfpipe.
True/False?

6 Your body produces adrenaline to
- a) stop you from feeling sick
- b) keep your body warm
- c) prepare your body for action
- d) slow your body down

7 A *wake* is the trail of water speedboats leave behind them.
True/False?

8 A *dirt dive* is a
- a) bungee stunt
- b) practice skydiving trick performed on the ground
- c) bike race on a dirt track
- d) dive that lands in the dirt

9 A *thrusty* is a special snow tyre for mountain bikes.
True/False?

10 A *fakie* is when you
- a) do a stunt and land facing backwards
- b) pretend to do a stunt
- c) do an awesome trick
- d) do a stunt and land facing the front

Answers

1 c)
2 True
3 a)
4 d)
5 False
6 c)
7 True
8 b)
9 False
10 a)

Glossary

adrenaline A chemical your body sends into your blood, when excited. This makes your heart beat faster and increases the amount of sugar in your blood.

aerial Something moving or happening in the air.

dehydration Excessive loss of water or fluid.

flexibility The ability to be easily bent or stretched.

freestyle A style which allows the performer to choose which style or method, or which movement to perform.

harnessed Strapped to something for safety.

hurtle To rush violently and noisily at high speed.

karabiner A metal safety device used in rock climbing.

noseslide To slide down or along something with the front of the board first.

reflexes A sudden unexpected physical reaction. An automatic response when a nerve is activated.

soar To rise in height through the air.

vert A ramp with vertical sides used for sporting, normally skateboards or BMX bikes.

wake The waves of water left behind an object moving in water.

Index